WENDY DALRYMPLE

Cadaver Bone

First edition

Editing by Candace Nola
Cover art by Wendy Dalrymple

This book was professionally typeset on Reedsy.
Find out more at reedsy.com

Contents

Preface

Content Warnings listed in the afterward at the end of this manuscript.

Acknowledgement

Thank you to Candace Nola, my go-to editor, cheerleader and friend.

Thank you to my beta reader and bestie, Jenna Dietzer. I couldn't do this author thing without you.

Thank you to Grace R. Reynolds for helping push me through the final draft of this and for always sending me next level reels and memes.

Thank you to my reviewers and author friends Heather Paul, Kirsten Craig, Bon the Witch, Damien Casey, Adam Hulse at Infested Publishing, Joey Powell at Mad Axe Media and Tasha Reynolds at The Sinister Scoop for taking the time to read advanced copies. Your friendship and readership are so valued and important to me.

And thank you to every reader who has ever taken a chance on my work and spent time with my words. Readers make indie publishing possible!

Chapter 1

General anesthesia should be a sugar-coated trip on a pink cloud, floating over silky marshmallow valleys under whipped cream skies — an easy segway from the stark reality of life to a disco dreamland where anything is possible. Knock me out and send me soaring over crystal castles through bubblegum skies, second star to the right and straight on 'til morning. Keep me comfortably numb and unaware under a purple haze of cotton candy flavored gas and never let me wake again. If only going under the knife was a never-ending effervescent dream. Instead, sedation was more like an instant and forgetful sleep that only led to a bleak, waking nightmare.

I had hoped to avoid knee surgery altogether after the accident. The whole situation was quite ironic, actually. There I was, forcing myself to get active again, trying to stay healthy by jogging and cutting back on my beloved carbohydrates. Instead, I twisted my ankle on an uneven bit of pavement, fell and tore my ACL. In the past, I would have just powered through an injury or illness, but no amount of ice, ibuprofen, or denial would fix my shredded ligament. I had to admit that a piece of my body had been destroyed, and this time, medical intervention was the only way I could heal.

When I awoke from the procedure, there were no glittery baby-faced angels or soft pink rose petals waiting for me on the other side of the operating table. No reassuring smiles from loved ones or calming music to ease me back into the waking world. Instead, I was met by a no-nonsense woman named Brenda with a severe haircut and a short temper. I was still too drugged up to care that her bedside manner was non-existent as she clacked away at her keyboard and made the occasional sniffling noise.

"We're going to monitor you for a few more minutes," she said. "I just need to finish up your paperwork and then Mr. Reyes can take you home."

My eyelids fluttered toward the acoustical tile ceiling as I fought against fuzzy thoughts and heavy limbs. I was aware of a new ache in my knee and the weight of my body pressing into the hospital bed, as well as the scratchy sensation of the bleached white sheet someone had pulled up to my chin. After who knows how long, Brenda checked the dressing on my knee one last time and she and two other nurses helped ease me off of the bed and into a wheelchair.

I hated the feeling of being out of control, especially when it came to my body. I hated feeling helpless and vulnerable and needing assistance. Mostly, I hated the fact that I wouldn't be able to be active again in the way that I wanted for a full year or more. If my accident proved one thing, it was that my mobility and independence were something I squandered and took for granted until I no longer had it.

"There's my princess." Dex stood up as Brenda wheeled me into the waiting room. Once again, I was glad to still be too drugged up to care about much of anything. I didn't like it when he called me princess. Still, I was happy to see a familiar face. My fiancé's handsome features were etched with worry. Dark circles rimmed his eyes and day-old scruff shadowed his jawline.

"Here are her discharge papers and after-care instructions. She'll need to be back in a week for a follow up." The nurse spoke to Dex as if I wasn't there. He left to start the car, and the nurse leaned down to face me. She pulled a ghoulish-looking smile and spoke in a condescending tone. "You'll be just fine."

Fine. Yeah, right.

I waited on the curb outside the clinic with the brusque nurse, wincing as the midday sun assaulted my eyes. It was only March, but in South Florida, warm weather sank its claws in early and held tight until November. Waves of heat radiated off the freshly paved blacktop, and the strong, tarry aroma caused my stomach to feel queasier than it already was. Dex pulled up to the curb, and I focused on Brenda's strong arms as she loaded me into the passenger seat of his car. The peacock blue polyester material of her scrubs felt rough against my skin, and the golden Gulf Coast Orthopedic embroidery seemed frayed and dull against her breast. Peacock blue and gold were the same colors I had picked out for my bridesmaids' gowns. I let out a dark chuckle at the thought.

"What's so funny?" Dex waved to Brenda as he pulled away.

My weakened body melted into the hot passenger seat, and I was grateful for the frigid air conditioning as it blasted me in the face. I licked my dry lips, my tongue an unwilling, desiccated slug as I struggled to speak. I let out another mad laugh and flopped my head to the side to face Dex.

"Brenda was dressed like one of my bridesmaids."

"Who?"

"The nurse," I said. "She wasn't very nice."

"Mia, we talked about this." Dex threw me an annoyed glance and scoffed. "No worrying about wedding stuff until after you heal."

"I'm not worrying," I said, my words slurring. "You're worrying."

I let out a shallow breath, closed my eyes and focused on the sound of tires whizzing over asphalt. The world swayed as Dex turned left, right, left, his car spinning me into whiplash circles like the eggbeater rides at the fair. I suddenly wished that I had asked my mother to pick me up after surgery instead of Dex. She would have been kinder and taken more care around the corners. But this was what fiancé's were supposed to do, right? We're supposed to take care of each other in sickness and in health and all that. I was well past the age of calling upon my parents for help, anyway. But as Dex muttered under his breath about paperwork and scheduling physical therapy sessions, I couldn't dismiss the feeling that my future husband might not be up to the task of caregiving.

"I was going to stop and get some burgers for lunch. Want anything?" He reached over and placed his hand on top of mine. My stomach flipped as his tire dipped into a pothole.

"No. I just wanna get home."

"Oh. Okay." Dex squeezed my hand. "The nurse said someone will come by this afternoon to deliver your therapy stuff."

"Great."

Dex continued his rollercoaster drive home, occasionally going over a bump too fast and sending searing stabs to the site of my incision. My clarity was beginning to return as I turned my attention from Dex to my newly operated on knee. The idea that I had been cut open and repaired, that strangers had access to my body while I was unconscious, all made me uneasy. Even though the procedure to repair my knee seemed simple enough, it sounded brutal, and I would have preferred to skip it. At my last appointment, the orthopedic surgeon explained to me that they would take part of my kneecap to reconstruct the ACL to repair my knee. I imagined her shaving off thin strips of white bone with a carrot peeler and replacing the material over my ruined ligaments, securing them in place with stainless steel pins. How long would my repair last? Would I ever really feel the same again?

When we arrived at our new house fifteen minutes later, I was immediately grateful I no longer had to face a third-floor walk-up. It had taken all of my savings and over a year of stalking real estate listings to move out of our apartment building and secure a quaint, over-priced single family starter home. Walking up and down multiple flights of stairs every day would have been impossible in my current state, and there wasn't any elevator access in our complex. Before the accident, I went from obsessively pouring over home prices, mortgage calculators and insurance packages, to scrolling bridal websites and wedding decor inspiration boards. I was sure that after the wedding we would be ready to start a family, and then I would transfer my need to obsess about wedding cakes and dresses to maternity websites and parenting boards. I had always been a planner and a dreamer, but no amount of planning and researching could have prepared me for being injured. I liked to have life mapped out and predictable, and having to waste time healing after an injury didn't fit into that.

Dex grabbed the pair of crutches we had packed in the car earlier that morning and helped me get out of the car. I could tell that whatever meds they had pumped into me were definitely beginning to wear off as the very weight of my dangling leg caused my knee to flame and pulse. Even with the heavy-duty brace, it felt like my leg was going to fall off and snap apart. The image of my leg separating in two, the joint snapping and meat tearing away like a chicken wing flashed before my eyes as I tried to focus on getting inside the house. I needed to lay down. I needed soft pillows, elevation, medication, and ice. Reality sucked and what I really wanted was to be knocked out again, so I didn't have to deal with anything at all.

With a lot of effort and a significant amount of pain, Dex shuttled me from the car to the house and onto our living room sofa. He propped me up, helped elevate my leg and got me a glass of water as I attempted to get comfortable. I leaned back on the couch, cursing myself for getting into this situation as Dex shuffled through my paperwork.

"Hmm. That's odd."

"What?"

"Don't worry about it." Dex said, stuffing the papers into a kitchen drawer.

As the drawer shut, something heavy clattered to the floor from the direction of the garage. I flinched, the loud sound causing my entire body to tense up. The movement caused me to accidentally straighten my leg, and fresh darts of sharp pain bloomed at my knee.

"What was that?" I winced, repositioning my knee.

"A racoon probably got into the garage again," he sighed. "I'll go check it out."

Dex disappeared into the garage as I leaned into the sofa and closed my eyes. I wanted to sleep until all of this was over; hibernate in my cave like a bear and emerge in the spring to start life anew. I would unwrap my bandage like a butterfly bursting from its cocoon, my injured limb restored and better than before. I couldn't just lay back and relax though. Recovery was going to take a lot of time, patience, pain, and work. I began to drift off again when Dex returned from the garage with a puzzled look on his face.

"Babe, did you accidentally run over my clubs or something?"

My eyes flashed open. "No. I haven't been able to drive since the accident, remember?"

"Oh. Right." Dex let out a sigh and ran a hand through his crop of dark, glossy curls.

"What's up? Did something happen?"

"My golf bag was knocked over in the garage. Every single one of my clubs was bent in half."

I frowned. "Are you sure?"

His eyes widened and blood rushed to his tanned cheeks as his lips pulled into a sneer. "Yes, I'm sure! My brand new nine-iron is totally fucked!"

"Hey, don't shout at me!" I shifted my position on the couch and a sharp stab ripped through my knee. "Ah, fuck!"

"Mia, you're not supposed to straighten it." Dex reached for me, and I swatted his hand away. "Let me help you."

I closed my eyes and exhaled a slow, ragged breath. These next few weeks were going to be hell. "I'm sorry your golf clubs were damaged, but I had nothing to do with it."

Dex hovered over me with his hands on his hips as a thick, heavy silence fell between us. It seemed like since we became engaged, things were more tense than ever. The wedding, the house, the injury; it was a lot of strain to put on our relationship. I tried to think of the last time we'd had fun together. I couldn't remember.

"Look, maybe it would be better if I just recuperated at my parents' house. I could..."

BANG. BANG. BANG.

But before I could finish my sentence, there was someone at the door.

Chapter 2

When I was a girl, I had envisioned that my future home would be a facsimile of my Barbie dream house. Magenta walls inside and out. Crystal chandeliers. Plush purple velvet chaise lounges. Floral curtains with lace accents and soft white carpets as far as the eye could see.

The house that Dex and I shared was far from that pretty pink dream. We begrudgingly came to a compromise when we bought the little 3-bedroom, 2-bathroom bungalow, decorating the modest space with a bland conglomeration of our things. Our living room featured a gray microfiber sofa, a wooden coffee table with matching television console and an abstract painting of the beach next to framed photos of us from early in our relationship. None of the furniture or decor suited either of our tastes; they were simply things that we picked out because we thought they made sense. As the technician arrived later that day with my physical therapy machines, I found myself embarrassed by the mediocrity of our home.

BANG. BANG. BANG.

"Wow, that was fast," Dex said, opening the front door.

Jayla, the medical equipment technician, was a pretty woman near my age with sparkling eyes and a killer figure. She worked fast to set up the machines in our living room, each of them designed to help with my physical therapy in a different way. One machine featured a built-in ice pad that would apply a cooling pack to my knee every few hours. The other machine was designed to slowly and gently move my leg position over time so that I would be able to regain full range of motion. Both of the machines were ugly and loud and clunky, but I was happy to have them.

"So, Mia, just make sure that this switch is flipped before you turn it on, okay?" Jayla smiled at me and dug into her pocket. She pulled out a business card and extended it toward me. "If you can't get something to work, just call me and I'll come out and check on the machine."

"I got it." Dex snatched the card from Jayla's hand. "I'm sure we'll figure things out okay."

I frowned as he tucked the business card into the back pocket of his pants. Dex was a good six inches taller than our guest, and I couldn't be sure, but for a moment, it could swear he was peering down the top of her scrubs. She crossed her arms at her chest and met my gaze with a 'is this guy for real?' expression.

"Take care of yourself," she said, pursing her lips. "I'll show myself out."

"Thank you, Jayla." I called.

The front door closed before I could get the entire sentence out. I turned to Dex and scowled as he stared out the front picture window and watched her get into her car.

"Hey," I said, half shouting.

"Huh?" Dex shook his head and tore away from his view. "What?"

"Could you get me my laptop and a glass of water?" I asked. "Please?"

"What do you need your laptop for?"

I sighed. "I just want to look up some things."

"Okay," Dex said, walking toward our office. "I already know what you're going to do, though."

"What? Ow." I winced, accidentally turning my leg the wrong way again.

"You're going to get all stressed out over wedding stuff." Dex emerged from our office with my laptop. "You're going to freak out because you can't find the right color napkins or something."

"No, I'm not," I said. "I just wanted to look up some information about my knee surgery. It hurts way worse than I thought it would."

"It's surgery." Dex shook his head and handed me the laptop. "It's supposed to hurt."

"But not like this," I said. "Fuck."

"Hold on. I'll go see if it's time for one of your painkillers." Dex turned and stomped toward the kitchen, huffing all the way like an angry little boy. I flinched as one of the cabinet doors slammed, followed by the sound of our fridge water dispenser. He returned a moment later with a glass of tepid water in one hand and two white pills in the other.

"Here." Dex gave me the glass and placed the pills in the palm of my hand. "I'm going out. There's nothing to eat here. Do you want me to get you something?"

I shook my head. "I'm not hungry yet."

"Okay, I'll be back in a bit."

Dex slipped out the front door and my hands and jaw instantly unclenched. I popped the pills in my mouth and swallowed them down, grateful for the painkillers. The inflamed cells in my body vibrated with every door slam or audible shout. I was eager for a moment of peace and quiet, and if I was being honest with myself, it was a relief for him to leave. So long as Dex was angrily stomping around the house, I couldn't relax. It hadn't always been this way.

There was once a time when I wanted to spend every moment with my fiancé. Weeknights cooking dinner together. Late Saturday nights dancing at the club, followed by lazy Sunday morning brunches. Weekends spent at the beach or at the golf course. I didn't even like golfing, but I liked being with him and riding around in the golf cart. When had we stopped being each other's best friend? After he proposed, I thought planning our future would only bring us closer together. But between buying the house, planning the wedding and now my injury, he seemed more distant than ever before. I just needed to hold out and put on a good face until I was healed and we were married. After that, everything would be just as it was supposed to be.

My pain-addled thoughts turned from wedding planning to ACL replacement research. I knew that I wouldn't feel like myself after the surgery, but my gut told me that I should ask more questions. Something didn't feel right about the procedure, but I couldn't put my finger on it. Even though the internet probably didn't have the answer, I felt compelled to look, anyway. I flipped the laptop open and typed "ACL replacement surgery" into the search bar, eager for some reassurance. It had been important for me to know as much as possible about my surgery, but all the YouTube videos and WebMD searches could never have prepared me for the post-op reality. I didn't know what I was looking for, but I couldn't just sit back and wonder. My research session didn't last long, though, before my thoughts became fuzzy and my eyelids began to droop.

My head lolled back, and I melted into the couch, submitting to the sedative power of my painkillers. I let go of myself as the heat of the laptop spread across my hips and up to my chest, pressing down on me like a warm, weighted blanket. My repaired knee pulsed at the operation site as though it had its own heartbeat, the rhythm intensifying with every beat. The warmth spread to my limbs, climbed up my neck and sunk into my veins as my knee throbbed harder and faster. The heat radiated through me, masking my face and climbing into my skull as a voice, clear as day, echoed through my mind.

Mine. Mine. Mine.

A fiery hand wrapped around my throat and squeezed. My eyes popped open as I sputtered against the pressure, gasping for air. My arms flailed out in front of me, expecting to push away a man in a ski mask or a stranger, possibly even Dex. But there was nothing. I clawed at my throat and choked as the hot fingers released their grip. My lungs were on fire as I greedily gulped a breath of air.

"Dex?" I sat up and my laptop fell to the floor with a thunk. My head whipped around as I searched the living room for an intruder or any sign of disturbance, but there was nothing. The house was still and silent as I scrambled to find my phone, my heart slapping against my chest. I swiped at the glass screen, ready to call 9-1-1 when the front door opened.

"Hey." Dex removed his sunglasses and regarded me with wide eyes. "Are you okay?"

"Someone was here," I said, my words stifled against a building sob. I rubbed the raw skin on my neck and I swallowed. It was still hot to the touch. "Someone was *choking* me."

"Are you sure?" Dex squinted and gave me a half-smile, half frown. "I locked everything up before I left."

"Yes! Go look!"

"Okay, okay." Dex placed a greasy fast-food bag on our entryway table. The aroma of French fries and seared meat wafted into the room with him as he breezed past the couch. I held back tears as he searched our small home from room to room, finally ending back up in the living room.

"Babe, there's no one here," he said. "You were probably having a night terror or something. Pain meds are known to cause hallucinations."

"This wasn't a hallucination! I felt it." I rubbed the raw skin on my neck. "Someone was here, and they were *hurting* me."

"Well, what do you want me to do?" Dex threw up his arms and let out an exasperated sigh. "Call the cops?"

"No, but I..."

"*Mia.*" Dex groaned and reached down next to the couch. He picked up the laptop and placed it on our coffee table. "You gotta be more careful. This could have broken."

I blinked in disbelief as Dex grabbed his bag of fast food and sat on the opposite side of the couch. I was still afraid, but another emotion was edging away the fear. Anger. How could he just sit there and eat French fries when I had been attacked?

"You're not going to do anything?"

"It's been a long day, Mia." Dex sighed and crammed a handful of fries into his mouth.

"Unbelievable," I said, swiping at my phone. "I'm calling my mom."

"Good. Maybe she can calm you down," Dex stood up from the couch with his bag of food. "I'm going to finish my meal in the office."

"Fine!" Fresh tears sprung to the corner of my eyes as I punched in my mother's number. I felt like a child. Helpless. Hurt. Unable to take care of big girl problems on my own.

I second-guessed myself and ended the call before it even rang. I didn't want to burden my mother with my relationship problems, anyway. She would just say *I told you so*, and that was the last thing I needed.

I leaned back on the couch as tears streamed down my cheeks. Everything hurt. My head. My heart. My fucking *knee*. I was stuck on this couch, scared and alone, but not really alone. Injuring my knee was the worst thing that could have happened possibly at that time in my life. I just wanted my body back. I wanted life to be the way it was before. Easy. Perfect. Everything I ever wanted and more.

Chapter 3

Dex was kinder to me after those first few bumpy post-op hours at home. Initially, I was angry about his behavior, but I couldn't blame him for being short with me. I knew that I wasn't an easy person to get along with. Obsessive. Overly emotional. I'm sure I wasn't a model patient either in those early hours after my surgery. Still, we worked through it and finally found a rhythm together as I forced myself to relax and heal.

I was back to work after a few days of recuperating, thankfully, from the comfort of my couch. My position as a project manager for a tech company paid well but zapped all of my mental energy. Planning the wedding had become my creative outlet, where I could lose myself for hours choosing colors schemes, researching table centerpieces and designing invitations. Every penny spent on the wedding was worth it, as was every missed hour of sleep searching for vendors and making DJ playlists. I needed to focus my energy on recovering so I could walk myself down the aisle in the hand-embroidered vintage wedding gown I purchased that cost more than my first car.

After work every day, Dex helped me shower and dress, and if he was too tired to cook, he got takeout delivered. He also reminded me when it was time to do my at-home physical therapy with the machines Jayla had set up, and helped me remember to take my pain medication. When he couldn't keep up with the housework, he even hired someone to come in and help clean. I didn't feel comfortable having strangers in my home, especially while I was working and recovering, but I didn't have much choice.

The pain in my knee was persistent and, at times, alarming. I couldn't move it the wrong way, and I couldn't move too fast, or I would pay dearly. I knew as part of my therapy that I needed to put pressure on my leg eventually, but every time I tried, it felt like a steak knife was jabbed into my kneecap. Medication and ice compresses only dulled the sharp, throbbing pain. I couldn't shake the feeling that something was wrong, despite Dex and my mother and anyone else I talked to brushing off my concerns.

After a few days of recovery had passed, I was dying to leave the house. I hated being cooped up with only my gray walls and gray furniture to look at. I had reached the end of Netflix's new releases and was bored with every other possible form of indoor entertainment. As usual, I wanted to be prepared for my follow-up appointment and needed some answers. Why was I hurting so much? Was there anything I could do to speed up my recovery? How long would I have to wear my leg brace? I realized that I hadn't even gone over my discharge papers to see what my after care should look like. I trusted Dex to get my care information right, but now I wasn't so sure.

The Sunday morning before my follow-up appointment, I woke up on the couch in agony. The sound of Dex's buzz-saw snores echoed down the hall from our bedroom, and I knew that I was on my own for breakfast. I grabbed my crutches and eased toward the kitchen in search of painkillers and water, my knee screaming with every movement. I found the bottle of painkillers, woefully counting how few I had left. What would happen when they were all gone? Would my doctor prescribe me more, or hopefully, something better?

I swallowed the pills and an entire glass of water as my gaze landed on a manilla folder near the sink. My white and yellow discharge papers peeked out from inside the thick stack. I grabbed the folder, tucked it under my arm, and maneuvered back toward the couch. Just before I made it, the folder slipped out from under my arm, sending the paperwork fluttering to the floor.

"Fuck!"

I tossed the crutches to the side and lowered myself back on the couch. Some of the papers were just out of reach, but I tried to pick up as many pieces of paper as I could, anyway. The first page I gathered was an itemized horizontal list of the procedures and medications given to me during the operation. I snorted at the outrageous pre-insurance price tag of my damaged knee. It cost almost as much out of pocket to fix my knee as it did to rent out the country club for our wedding.

Next, I read a page that listed my discharge information. I noted Jayla's name and the phone number to the equipment rental company at the top. The price tag for the equipment rental was listed as well, and I nearly choked as I read the invoice. Everything checked out, though; I was getting the right amount of medication at the right time. Nothing in the discharge papers seemed off until I spotted a navy-blue postcard that had fluttered from the packet. I picked up the postcard and stared at it for a full minute before registering the words printed on the front.

CADAVER MATERIAL RECIPIENT

The material used in your procedure has been harvested from a donor cadaver.
You may send an anonymous email to the family of the deceased to express how the donation of this cadaver material has impacted your life to the following email:
donor@cadaverbank.org
Please refer to the following reference number when sending your message, and refrain from adding personal information, including your name, age, and location.
REF: 845G32R0A

My hand trembled as I read the card again and again. Cadaver material? Donor? Were there body parts from a fucking corpse sewed into my body? How could this have happened? The thought alone caused watery bile to rise in my throat. I caught my breath and massaged my temples. What did this mean? Dex had to know.

"Dex?" I called out. "Dex!"

His steady snoring halted with a snort, followed by a groan and the metallic crunch of mattress springs. A moment later, my fiancé emerged from the darkened hallway wide-eyed and dressed only in his boxers.

"What happened? Are you okay?"

"Did you know about this?" I held up the postcard, my blood boiling.

His worried features relaxed as he eyed the donation recipient card. He ran a hand through his hair and let out a sigh. "Jesus, Mia. I thought you were hurt."

"When were you gonna tell me I have body parts from a dead person in my knee?"

Dex shook his head. "I was going to let the doctor tell you

at your follow-up tomorrow. You were too upset that first day back home, and I didn't know what to say."

"I'm gonna be sick." This time, a little bile did manage to bubble up into my mouth. My esophagus burned as I swallowed it back down. "I didn't consent to this. How could you let them do that to me?"

"Your original surgery failed," Dex said. "They asked me to make a decision for you and they had the donation material ready. I figured it would be better than not getting it fixed at all."

"I don't know what to say." I clenched my jaw as hot tears formed at the corner of my eyes. I felt like I had been lied to. Betrayed. Infantilized. Yes, I was upset that something had happened to me without my consent. But I wasn't a baby. He didn't need to hide things from me. I deserved to know and finding out this way felt awful.

"Dammit, Mia, enough with the tears," Dex said, turning toward the bathroom. "It's always theatrics with you."

"Theatrics!" I shouted. "How the fuck would you feel if you had goddamn dead people inside of you?"

Dex shut the bathroom door. I buried my face in my hands, trying my hardest not to cry. Maybe this would finally be it. The last straw. If our relationship was this tumultuous all through knee surgery, was our wedding even worth going through with? Is this what our life together would be like if we decided to start a family? All the time and money and heart I had put into planning our wedding would be wasted if we gave up now. If I stayed, things might never change, and I would resign myself to a life of settling for something that didn't feel right. Either way, I would lose.

A few moments later, Dex emerged from the bathroom and

stomped back toward our bedroom. Dresser drawers opened and shut, and after a few minutes, he came out wearing a polo shirt and his golf shorts.

"Where are you going?"

Dex threw me an icy glance as he picked up his car keys from the front entry table. "I'm going to go hit some balls and blow off some steam."

"You're going to just leave me here?"

"It's Sunday. I need to get the fuck out of here. If you need anything, you can call your mom." Dex opened the front door and shut it behind him without saying another word.

"Asshole!" I shouted at the door. My attempts at not crying failed then, as I let out a bitter sob. I was hurt and alone. I didn't want to feel like this anymore. I didn't want to feel anything at all.

I got up and walked myself to the kitchen on crutches, the pain in my knee just as intense as before. I needed something else to take off the edge, to make the pain stop. Even though I wasn't due for more pain medication for another six hours, I took an extra dose. Fuck it. I wished that I had never tried to start jogging again. I wished that I was a different person, less emotional. I wished that I knew what to say to make everything right.

When I returned to my nest on the couch, I picked up my phone and called my mother. Dex had won. He was right. I couldn't do anything on my own. The phone rang a half dozen times before going straight to voicemail.

"Hi, this is Michelle," my mother's chirpy voice rang in my ear. "Leave me a message and I'll get right back!"

BEEP.

"Hey Mom," I sniffled into the phone. "I, um. I just wanted

to say hi. I haven't seen you since my surgery and it's been kind of hard. Dex is a big help, but he's out golfing today. Anyway, if you aren't busy, it would be nice if you could stop by. Love you."

I pressed the END CALL button on the glass and stared back at my reflection in the black mirror of my phone, my disheveled hair sticking out in unruly wisps around my head. How had I become this pathetic person? I used to be independent. Stronger. Now I was all alone, miserable and stuck inside a house I hated. It was still early, but perhaps I could call my best friend Ashley. She was always there to listen.

But before I was able to place the call to my friend, my reflection began to shift. The sockets of my eyes hollowed, and the tip of my nose fell away, disintegrating like sand. My noseless face made me look like a villain in a post-apocalyptic story. But it was my mouth that terrified me the most. My lips pulled back along my receding gum line to expose two perfect rows of teeth. My dark reflection smiled back at me in a ghoulish sort of way.

Mine. Mine. Mine.

I screamed as the black screen disappeared and my skeletal reflection was replaced by the smiling image of my mother. I sucked in a shuddered breath, pushed the green ACCEPT CALL button, and answered the phone.

"Mom." I sobbed, unable to control myself.

"Sweetie! Oh, my word, are you okay?" My mother's alarmed voice only broke my heart more. I was such a fuckup. First Dex and now my mom. I never wanted to be a burden to anyone, never wanted to ask for help. But something was wrong, and I knew I couldn't do this on my own. I sucked up my pride, wiped my teary eyes, and whispered into the phone.

"Can you come over, please?"

Chapter 4

I spent the night at my childhood home after Dex stormed out. While he was at the driving range, my mother came over to help pack my things as I tearfully unloaded everything that had happened on her. She hauled my rehabilitation machines to her car as I sobbed and stashed my medications, laptop and clothes into the suitcase I had bought for our honeymoon. I felt ashamed and embarrassed, like I was running away. I also felt relieved. At least I could be comfortable back at home with my parents. I could get the care that I needed from people who loved me.

The walls in my old bedroom used to be covered in a cream and pink ribbon wallpaper when I was a teenager. After I moved out, my parents painted the walls a dark slate hue, just as gray and bland as my living room back home. My room had long ago been turned into a guest bedroom/office, but it still felt like mine in a lot of ways. My childhood dresser served as a TV stand, and my bed frame was still there as well. All of my posters and personal items were gone, but as I laid in the bed and stared at the ceiling, I felt like a teenager all over again. Trapped. Loved. Home.

By the time I was settled in, a massive headache had taken up residence inside my skull. It was afternoon, and I hadn't eaten all day, and my nonstop crying jags certainly didn't help ease my throbbing brain either. My mother brought me soup and a sandwich as I listlessly watched my phone, waiting for Dex to call. I had left him a note explaining where I was and to please leave me alone, but part of me wanted him to call, anyway. It wouldn't fix things, but I knew that a big, romantic gesture would be all it would take to get me back home. I needed to feel wanted, and Dex hadn't made me feel that way in a long time.

Every time I glanced at my silent phone, the memory of my skull-like features flashed before my eyes. Perhaps it was the medication or being under stress, but the macabre visual disturbance, well... disturbed me. I didn't want to worry my mother, but planned to mention what I was experiencing to my doctor at the follow-up appointment. More importantly, I wanted to know about the cadaver material that had been grafted onto my bone. Had I signed something in the paperwork stating that the physicians were allowed to use donor material? I certainly didn't remember them talking about using cadaver tissue during pre-op visits, and if that information was in the fine print of the medical release forms, then I missed it.

Dex honored the boundary I had set and didn't call or text me that first night. I didn't know if I appreciated that fact, or if his silence angered me even more. I wanted him to grovel and apologize; to promise to work with me so we could get our relationship back on track. Instead of planning for my wedding with my fiancé, I spent the rest of the evening eating pizza with my mom and dad and watching sitcom reruns in the living room.

I couldn't bring myself to talk to my parents about what was bothering me, both my problems with Dex and the donor material now permanently attached to my knee. Mom was squeamish about graphic bodily things, and my father never liked Dex from day one, so neither of those conversations wouldn't have gone well, anyway. Even though I was miserable, at least I could veg out with junk food and comfort TV from the safety of their couch and pretend that my life wasn't in shambles.

That night, after my parents turned in, I was left to my own devices. I returned to my bedroom and sat on the bed, spinning my engagement ring on my left hand. It was a nice ring. Expensive. At that moment, I wanted to pull it off my hand and chuck it across the room, but I couldn't. My hands had become swollen after the surgery and I couldn't get my ring past the knuckle. Panic began to rise in my throat as I pondered about what might happen if I couldn't get it off. What if this ring, that was supposed to be a symbol of our everlasting love and commitment, became a torture device instead? What if my finger became so swollen and engrossed with blood around the metallic band that it turned black and fell off?

I shook off the gruesome thought and turned my attention instead to my old closet. Nostalgia swept over me as I uncovered a box of things I had left behind when I moved out. Forgotten stuffed animals. A girl scout uniform in a plastic garment bag. A clear plastic storage box with an assortment of random toys. But it was my high school yearbooks that caught my eye.

I grabbed the volume from my senior year from the top shelf of the closet, using my free arm to balance on my crutches. It had been a long time since I cracked the spine on the massive hardcover book. I made myself comfortable in bed and opened the cover, smiling at the dozens and dozens of signatures and inscriptions inside. High school was a happy time for me; I was popular and had so many friends. On the days I was feeling particularly cruel to myself, my intrusive thoughts would tell me that I was one of those girls who peaked in high school. My relationship with Dex proved all that wrong, though. Girls who peaked in high school didn't have good jobs, great boyfriends, and nice houses. Planning my wedding proved that I had it all. I made it, and there were even more good things to come. Right?

Unsurprisingly, photos of my best friend Ashley and I dominated the front half of the yearbook. I was a cheerleader in high school and Ashley was an editor on the yearbooks, so the pages were filled with more of our memories than those of the other kids. I flipped past photos of me with my high school boyfriend, Shane, his eyes and mouth scribbled out in permanent marker. Nearly every page I had written something nasty about another student. When you're seventeen, you don't think about other people's needs and existence in the same way, but as an adult, looking back at those pages made me cringe. Had I always been so self-centered? Why had I been so mean and hateful? Was I still this horrible to other people?

I picked up my phone and flicked the screen to my text messages. Still nothing from Dex. I scrolled down to Ashley's name and sent her a 'hey' text. When was the last time I had heard her voice or seen her in person? She texted to check in the day before my surgery, but I hadn't heard anything back since. Our relationship had once bordered on codependency, and now it was reduced to swapping Instagram reels and memes now and then. I had been wrapped up in my own life and Dex for so long now, I forgot what it was like to just hang out with friends. The ellipses on the screen lit up, indicating she was texting me something back, but then, after a moment, it stopped. Nothing. I couldn't even get a text back or a call from my best friend. I was nothing. I was shit.

That night I finally fell asleep thinking about what my life could be like if I just decided to be brave and leave Dex for good.

Sure, I would lose tens of thousands of dollars spent on deposits for a wedding that wouldn't happen. There would be more fights, and we would have to put our home up for sale. Possibly lawyers would get involved, and I would have to live back at home with my parents for a while. I would be lonely and feel like a failure, but I would be free. The real question was whether or not I wanted to be free. I wasn't even sure I knew what true freedom would look like.

***

"Everything looks like it's healing up nicely. Do you have any questions?"

Dr. Matthias removed her reading glasses and gave me a warm smile. My follow-up visit started out well, going over all the usual after care information. I glanced over at my mother as she dabbed her nose with a tissue. The doctor's office was cold, and I wished that I had brought a sweater as I shivered against the powerful air conditioning.

The post-op visit was the first chance for me to get a look at my healing knee. Since I came home from surgery, I had kept it wrapped up and in the big, clunky brace unless I was using one of the machines to ice or stretch it. From all the pain and throbbing I was experiencing, I expected the wound to be red, surrounded by swollen black and blue skin. Instead, there was a single vertical pink scar that ran the length of my kneecap and healthy-looking flesh.

"I'm still experiencing a lot of pain. Is that normal?"

"Well, some discomfort is normal after surgery," Dr. Matthias said. "Are the painkillers not helping?"

"Not really." I shifted in my seat and winced. "Is there anything else you could give me?"

Dr. Matthias glanced at my mother and then back at me again.

"Well, why don't we just give it a little more time, huh? Are you using your therapy machines correctly?"

"Yes," I said, heat blooming in my cheeks. I felt like a child again, getting scolded in the doctor's office while my mother looked on. "Actually, I had another question."

"Oh?"

"No one told me that I was given donor material during the surgery," I said. "I only found out days after the fact when I looked through my discharge papers."

"Donor material?" My mother frowned and tilted her head. "That sounds serious. Wouldn't she need to take anti-rejection medication for something like that?"

"No. With cadaver bone material, there's no exchange of DNA from donor to patient," Dr. Matthias explained. "It's so strange though, you should have been informed of the emergency procedure."

Dr. Matthias picked up my file and propped her reading glasses back onto the bridge of her nose. She rifled through the papers and then glanced back up at me. "Ah, here it is. It says here that your caregiver was informed and consented to the use of the donor material. We tried to perform the operation as planned, but sometimes these things happen."

"Really?" I pursed my lips. "I guess I just wished that I had been better prepped for the possibility of this happening. It was quite a shock to hear that I have a dead person's body parts in me now."

"It does sound rather morbid, I know," Dr. Matthias chuckled. "I really hope you can see it as the gift that it is, though. You were lucky that we had donor material available, or your knee wouldn't work anymore."

She was right. I was being a big baby about the whole thing.

Someone else had lost their loved one and was generous enough to donate their usable tendons to me. I needed to just push the idea out of my mind.

"It was a bit of a shock, but I *am* grateful," I said. "Thank you."

"Keep your chin up," Dr. Matthias said. "Just stick to your physical therapy and don't overdo it, and you'll be walking down the aisle all by yourself. When is the big day again?"

My heart blipped. The wedding. Was it even still going to happen? I glanced down at my engagement ring. Even though it was stuck, and I was pissed off at Dex, I honestly didn't have the heart to think about taking it off yet. I wasn't ready to admit that things were over. I wasn't in the mood to spill my entire personal life to my orthopedic surgeon, either.

"This fall," I said. "Around Halloween."

"How lovely." Dr. Matthias patted my shoulder. "We'll see you in a few weeks for another follow-up."

"Thank you, doctor." My mother stood and shook Dr. Matthias's hand. My already bruised ego took another hit as they exchanged strained smiles and another conspiratorial glance. Dr. Matthias felt sorry for my mother for having to deal with me, I knew. I was a difficult daughter, prone to dramatics and always in need of attention. Even my orthopedic surgeon could see that. Everyone could see that.

My knee still hurt, but everything else felt numb as I checked out of my appointment that afternoon. I had hoped to get some answers or at the very least some reassurance about my procedure, but instead, I was left feeling infantile and more confused. I wanted to be able to have a positive outlook and hope for the best. I wanted to reassure myself that I was just going through a tough time and that everything would work out.

As my mother followed me out of the doctor's office, I couldn't force myself to feel anything but self-pity and despair.

I glanced across the medical plaza parking lot toward our vehicle, eager to rest my throbbing leg. But when I spied my mother's SUV under the shade of a large oak, instead of a sigh of relief, I let out a gasp. Someone was leaning up against the hood of her car.

Watching. Waiting.

Chapter 5

Dex offered a forlorn expression shaded by heavy brows as he straightened up from his perch on my mother's car. His face was freshly shaved, and he was dressed in a crisp shirt and a pair of pants that I didn't recognize. A bouquet of red roses appeared from behind his back as we crossed the parking lot toward him, and an invisible fist punched my heart. As I met his gaze, something inside my brain snapped. Did I want to see him? Or did I want to punch him in the heart, too? I tipped my chin upward and tried my best to sound brave.

"I said I wanted you to leave me alone."

My mother exchanged a scowl with me and unlocked her car as he approached. The scent of his cologne traveled on the warm early morning breeze and my bruised heart ached. He cleared his throat and offered the flowers, which I accepted like a reflex. They were nice roses, the kind you get from an actual florist and not the grocery store. I brought them to my nose and inhaled.

"I remembered you had your follow up appointment today," he said. "I don't expect you to talk to me. I just wanted to bring you these and tell you I'm sorry."

"What are you sorry for?" I extended the bouquet back to him.

He stared at the flowers but didn't take them back. "I've been a real asshole. You're in a lot of pain, and I haven't been as good to you as you deserve. I know I need to work on my attitude. I don't blame you for wanting to take a break."

Damn. I brought the flowers back and held them to my chest as feel-good chemicals flooded my veins. It was almost as if he knew exactly what I wanted to hear. My mother started the car and opened the passenger door. It was time to leave.

"I've got to go."

"Here, let me help you." Dex opened up the back seat and took the crutches and flowers from me. He gently placed them in the back, closed the door, and helped me into the front passenger seat. My palm ached at the skin-on-skin contact. I hated how much I wanted his touch and felt a need for it. I buckled my seatbelt and gazed up at him, not sure if there was anything else to say.

"I'll stay away if that's what you want, but I'm ready to talk whenever you are. Home isn't the same without you, Mia."

"Thank you, Dex." My mother smiled. "We've got to be going, now."

"Bye." I gave him one last sidelong glance as he shut the door. My reflection in the window glass was pathetic as I stared back at him. Hollowed. Tired. Skeletal.

***

I asked Dex to come pick me up later that evening, because of course I did. Staying at my parents' house wasn't going to solve any of our problems, and the truth was, I got what I wanted. Dex apologized and groveled. He came for me. He showed up. He promised things would change. I wanted to believe him, one hundred percent. I wanted to get back to recovering at home, back to wedding planning, back to our happy future together. We packed up all of my things, including the box of my old toys and yearbooks, and headed back home. I was happy for a moment.

And yet, as he helped me onto my nest on the couch, a little thread of doubt wiggled in my gut.

That night, Dex and I shared a bottle of wine, and he showed me just how sorry he was. Dex had a high sex drive, but my injury had put a pause on our intimate time together, so it had been a while since we had come together physically. Even before I got hurt, our sheets had begun to cool a little. I shrugged off our lack of sex as being a natural relationship progression or a stress response. When you're in a relationship with someone for a long time, there can be dry spells and tough times. It would frustrate Dex when I was too tired after a long day of work or not feeling well enough to keep up with his physical needs. I knew I would have to do better in that department if I wanted us to be close again.

When we were finished and the bottle of wine was spent, Dex fell asleep next to me on the couch. I watched junk TV and my thoughts returned to the donated piece of human tissue surgically implanted in my knee. The informatio card had mentioned that I could send an anonymous message to the family of the donor material to thank them. It occurred to me that sending a message might be cathartic, not just for me, but for the donor's family. With so much weighing on me, I was willing to do just about anything to feel a little relief.

I grabbed my purse from the coffee table and found the donor card and the contact information. What would I say to the family of someone who has lost a loved one? They didn't care about me or my life, or that a piece of their family member now resided inside of me. Why would they? I knew that I couldn't give away any information about who I was or where I lived, so what else could I say? Still, I was wide awake and in pain while Dex snored beside me. I had nothing else to lose. I picked up my laptop, flipped the screen open, and pulled up my email server.

To: donor@cadaverbank.org
From: mia.hopkins@mail.com
Subject: REF: 845G32R0A

Dear Donor Family,

I don't really know what to say to convey my gratitude to you and your departed loved one. Your gracious donation was used in a surgery last week to help repair and reconstruct my damaged ACL. I injured my knee running, and because of your donation, I'll be able to walk down the aisle at my wedding this fall. More importantly, I'll be able to run again someday. Thank you again. This donation has impacted my life in more ways than you know.

Sincerely,
MH

Send. I hoped that adding my initials at the end wouldn't be too much, but I didn't know how else to sign off. Whoever was monitoring emails at the cadaver bank before sending them out to the families would probably edit out that kind of information, anyway.

The wedding. Would I really be able to walk myself down the aisle in just a few months? I had my doubts. Just as I was about to put my laptop away, a message notification pinged. I clicked over to the "I DO!" wedding planning website where a little red NEW MESSAGE bubble blipped next to my username. I always had a tab with the wedding planning website open on my laptop so that I could browse for ideas or ask questions on the message boards when work was slow. I opened my messages and cringed in expectation of what was likely waiting for me.

To: MiaLuvsDex
From: user987620934
Subject: fucking ugly fuck

I sighed and held my finger over the mouse pad. I knew I should just delete the message like all the other ones I had before. I thought that whoever had been trolling my "I DO!" account had long ago given up. For months after Dex and I got engaged, any time I would post a new inspiration board or ask a question in one of the chat rooms, a user with no photo and no name would come into my messages and spew hate at me. I reported the abuse to the "I DO!" moderators, and they were able to stop it for a while, but I guess they were back. Curiosity got the best of me, and I opened the message against my better judgment.

You are fucking gross, your sofucking ugly, youdon't deserve a man like that I hope your knee splits infuckingtwo when you walk down the aisle FUCKING BITCH!

Something in my brain clicked as I read the message. This wasn't a message from a random troll. I hadn't mentioned my knee injury anywhere online; not on the "I DO!" website, not on social media. Not anywhere. This wasn't just someone who didn't know me trying to get a rise out of whoever they could. This was personal.

My laptop screen went black, and I gasped. I had forgotten to charge it at my parents' house and didn't realize the battery was low. Panic rose up into my throat in hot waves as I thought of the words on that hateful message again and again. The light from the television illuminated my features in the dark, and my ghastly reflection peered back at me from the laptop screen again. Hollowed cheekbones and eye sockets. Thin lips that pulled away from the gums, exposing elongated teeth.

Mine. Mine. Mine.

A loud, droning whine pierced my ears and a lightning bolt of pain crept across my skull. I winced and fell back onto the couch, clutching my hands to my ears. The pain was too intense to bear, and it didn't take long for my body to give in. My eyes slammed closed and then there was darkness and nothing more.

Chapter 6

Gorgeous rays of sunshine kissed my cheeks and skimmed across my eyelids as morning dawned the following day. The windows were wide open, allowing an unusually pleasant spring breeze to blow into the living room. A mockingbird sang a pretty little tune as I stretched and willed myself back into the waking world. My headache was gone, and it was a brand-new day. Everything was bathed in golden sunlight, and I was a fairytale princess, ready to claim the life I always desired.

"Look who's awake."

Dex emerged from the kitchen with a tray of tea, biscuits and jam. My multivitamin and pain pills were even organized on a napkin for me. He laid the tray on the coffee table, bent down, and planted a kiss on the top of my head.

"I was going to make bacon and eggs, but I'm running late."

"No, that's okay. This is lovely," I said. "You have to go into the office today?"

"I told you, remember? They're making us go back three days a week now. So ridiculous, it's all just for show. You'll be okay though, won't you?"

"Right." I poured a cup of tea and held the warm mug against my chest. "Yeah, I'm sure I'll be fine. I have to log on to work soon myself."

"Great. I gotta get dressed."

Dex walked back toward our bedroom, leaving me with my tea and toast. I was going to be alone again. The idea of not having anyone nearby made me nervous, especially since I was still recovering and getting around on one good leg wasn't so easy. I could call my mother again, of course, but my pride couldn't take that hit. Not after I had just run back home to Dex.

"Maybe I'll see if Ashley wants to go out to lunch today," I called out. "I haven't seen her since before my surgery."

"Sounds good."

I picked up my phone and scrolled through my contacts list, landing on Ashley's number. My best friend had married her high school sweetheart and got down to the business of being a stay-at-home mom early. Now that her youngest child was in kindergarten, she had time during the day to herself again. We didn't get to hang out one-on-one as much as I would like, but she was always there to listen, and I was happily Auntie Mia to her kids.

M: I'm crawling out of my skin with boredom! Wanna go grab some tacos for lunch today?

It only took a few moments for the ellipsis to blip on my phone screen, followed by a response. Like me, my best friend almost always had her phone in her hand.

A: Duh, of course. Be at your place to pick you up at 12. I'm paying today, my treat.

M: Heart eyes emoji

I smiled and took another sip of tea. It was nice to have someone other than my parents, who I could always rely on.

"Mia, have you seen my wallet?" Dex called out to me. "I can't find it anywhere."

"Why would I know where your wallet is?" I asked.

"I don't know!" When Dex got stressed, his tone got shitty, and he was easily flustered. At least once a day, he misplaced something of his own and expected me to know where it was.

"Did you check the office? Sometimes you leave it there," I said, rolling my eyes.

Heavy footsteps sounded in the hall, followed by squeaking hinges as Dex opened the office door. "What the fuck?"

I sat up and put my teacup down. "What's wrong?"

Dex entered the living room, his features screwed up in a confused expression. He held out two halves of my 3" binder, the blue and white one I got from Target, designed especially for planning weddings. It had been ripped clean in half.

"My planner!"

"Why did you do that?" He handed me the shredded binder. "There's receipts and paperwork all over the office floor."

"Me? How could you think it was me?" I shouted as tears pricked the corners of my eyes. I loved that binder. It had a slot for everything. A folder for receipts from the florist, the caterers, the DJs. A place to write down potential wedding guests and other wedding to-do checklists. When it came to planning the wedding, I would be lost and disorganized without my binder.

"I know we had a fight, but Jesus, Mia." Dex ran his hands through his hair and let out an exasperated sigh. "You know what? I don't have time for this."

"I'm sorry. I don't know what happened," I said, my voice strained as I choked back tears. "Maybe someone broke in."

"No one broke in." Dex spotted his wallet on the entryway table next to his keys. He grabbed them both and gave me a sad, vacant look. "I'll see you after work."

He breezed past me and walked out the door as fat tears flowed down my cheeks. Maybe it had been a mistake to come home. Me and Dex. The wedding. My surgery. My whole life. It was all wrong. I melted back into the couch, crying as golden light bathed every inch of my body. For the first time in over a week, I didn't even think about the pain in my knee. The pain in my heart overshadowed everything else. I didn't care about work, or my recovery, or anything. I wanted relief. I wanted to die.

***

"You look like shit."

Ashley pushed her oversized glasses up on the top of her head and gave me a peck on the cheek as she entered my home later that day. She pressed a cup of my favorite coffee into my hand, a hazelnut latte, and I gave her a hug. As usual, Ashley was beautiful and vibrant, even with her brunette hair swept up in a bun and dressed casually in leggings and a loose tank top. She had always been the pretty friend when we were in school. As adults, that status hadn't changed.

"Thanks." I snorted. "I call this look *Depression Chic.*"

"No seriously. You're so pale. And skinny," Ashley frowned. "I know it's been a minute since I've seen you, but wow. You're really taking this whole wedding weight loss thing seriously."

"I think my pain meds are making me nauseous or something," I said. "And I haven't really been able to get out. I'll be happy to sit in the sun for a bit today."

"How long do you have for lunch break?"

"As long as I want," I said. "I took the day off. Dex and I got into a fight, and I couldn't focus on work."

"Again?" Ashley said, grabbing my purse. "What was it this time?"

I followed her out the door, steadier on my feet now and moving more fluidly with the crutches. My knee was secured in the brace like always, but that day, it felt better. Maybe my pain killers were finally working right.

"Just relationship stuff. You know how it is sometimes with you and Jason," I said.

"Oh yeah," Ashley said. "There's always something."

I had spent the morning crying and cleaning up the contents of my broken wedding binder in the office. I didn't want to tell Ashley about what was happening, or about my weekend with my parents. I knew what she would say, and I just wanted to have a nice lunch with my friend.

She helped me into her car and we drove to a nearby brunch place that we both loved. We grabbed a seat on the patio and each downed our "one and done" mimosas before our omelets came out. Ashley filled me in on her kids, her family, the new yoga class she was taking. She asked me about wedding stuff, but I brushed it off, not wanting to really talk about bridesmaid's gown fittings or hair appointments. I hadn't yet told her about the sordid details of my surgery either, but tactfully waited until she was one eating to bring it up. Ashley pushed her plate away and gave me a pitiful half smile, half frown.

"So, when will you have full range of motion in your knee again?" She asked.

"They said it will take up to a year to fully heal. I'm supposed to wear my brace for a while yet. Get this, though." I pulled out the donor card from my purse and passed it to her. "Have you ever heard of cadaver tissue donation?"

"No," she said, examining it and passing it back. "What's

that? Like tissues from dead people?"

"That's exactly what it is. Apparently, my initial knee surgery didn't go as planned. They were supposed to use a graft of my kneecap to fix the tendon, but it didn't work. They had to use donor material instead. This card has the ID number of the person it was donated from."

"That's wild," Ashley said. "Did you know they were going to do that?"

"Nope. They called Dex to get his approval during surgery while I was knocked out," I said. "I asked about it in my follow up and I was brushed off. The information about the possibility of using donor material is in the fine print I signed, but I would have appreciated a heads up about it."

"That seems like something that they should have definitely gone over with you," she said. "Can I see that card again?"

"Sure."

I handed the card back to her, and Ashley read the information again. "So, you can email the family who the donor material belongs to?"

"Yeah. It's supposed to be anonymous, though."

"Aren't you curious who it was?" Ashley said, her eyes sparkling.

"Not really," I said. "The less I know, the better. I just want to heal up and move on."

"What if it was, like, the tendon of an amazing athlete," she said. "You'll run even faster than ever now."

"*Stop.*" I rolled my eyes.

"Come on, you're not a little bit curious about your zombie knee?"

"Don't call it that!" A genuine belly laugh escaped from my lips. I couldn't remember the last time I laughed like that.

"For real though," Ashley said. "You know Stephen does dark web shit. He could figure out who your dead body parts belonged to, no sweat."

"Ash, I'm not going to ask your little brother to break the law for me."

"Why not? I do it all the time to get coupon discounts for my favorite retinol cream. That shit's expensive," she said. "Come on, let me see what I can find out."

"Sure. Why not?"

Ashley snapped a photo of the donor card with her phone, then handed the card back to me. "I'll send this to Stephen and see if he can find anything."

"Thanks. And thank you for picking me up. I needed this today."

"I did too. I feel like we barely get to see each other anymore," she said. "Ever since you started planning this wedding, you've been so stressed. I miss you."

"I know, I miss you, too. Things at home have been a little bumpy, especially after the accident, but it'll be over soon."

Ashley gave me that same half smile, half frown as the server came by with our check. She placed three twenties on the table to pay for the check and stood up. "What if it isn't over, though?"

"What do you mean?"

"I mean, what if Dex starts acting like a dick again?" She grabbed my crutches and helped me out of my chair. "You don't have to go through with the wedding, you know."

"Why would you say that?"

Ashley locked her gaze with mine. "I'm just saying. I support whatever you want to do, but if you feel like something isn't right, you can always back out."

"I don't want to back out," I said. "Dex and I will be fine."

Ashley nodded and broke away from my gaze. "Of course you will. I'm just worried, you know?"

"I know. I love you."

"I love you, too."

We left the restaurant, and I followed Ashley back to her car, walking faster than ever on my crutches. I felt like a whole new person. Maybe it was the mimosa or the sunshine. Maybe I was just feeling better after getting out of the house and talking to a friend. Either way, I was refreshed. Renewed. Ready to face what was waiting for me at home.

Chapter 7

That night before Dex got home, I did my best to clean up and make myself look presentable. I curled my hair, put on makeup and slipped into a curve-hugging dress. By then, I had become a pro at moving around with my crutches, and the pain in my knee wasn't nearly as intense. Cooking was still tricky, but I ordered steak dinners from Dex's favorite restaurant and set our dining room table with flowers and candles. Now that I was feeling more like myself again, I would be able to put some real effort into our relationship again. I was going to make things work with us. I had to.

Dex pulled into our driveway after 9 p.m. that night. Our dinner was cold, my hair was flat and my anger had returned. He walked into the front door, looking exhausted as he met my gaze. He dropped his wallet and keys in the dish by the front door and flopped on the couch.

"What are you all dressed up for?"

"Hi to you too," I said. "I cleaned up and ordered dinner."

"You did?" He glanced over at the dining room table. The taper candles that I had lit hours ago were reduced to drippy nubs. "Why didn't you say something?"

"I wanted to surprise you," I said. "I got steak dinners from Barbacoa."

"Aw, shit, Mia. I already ate." Dex leaned over and gave me a kiss. His breath smelled like beer and chicken wings. "Thank you, though."

"You didn't think to ask if I wanted to go to dinner?"

"My boss ordered food in for everyone," Dex said. "It's tax season. You know how it is. We had to finish up a big account before we could all go home."

"Right." I crossed my arms in front of my chest. "You can just take it for lunch tomorrow if you want, I guess."

"That would be great." Dex bit his lower lip and cocked his head to the side. "Please don't be upset with me, Mia. I'll make it up to you this weekend."

"How?"

"I don't know. What about cake tasting at Bon Vivant?"

My ears perked up. I had been trying to convince Dex to come to my favorite bakery with me for weeks to taste test cake samples for the wedding. He always had an excuse every time and wanted me to handle it on my own. He knew it was important to me that he come with and choose a flavor of cake we would both like. Maybe he really was trying to change.

"Then afterwards we can go have a nice dinner," he said. "Come on, Mimi. Please let me make it up to you."

Mimi. How long had it been since he called me that pet name? I didn't hate it quite as much as when he called me princess, but it still wasn't my favorite. Maybe he really did have a late work night. Maybe he really did want to make things up to me. I was too mentally and physically exhausted at that point to argue.

"Yeah, that would be nice."

"Did you have lunch with Ashley today?"

"Mhmm," I said. "It was good to see her. We hardly ever hang out anymore."

"What did you all talk about?"

"You know, stuff." I yawned. "I told her about the donor material that they used during the surgery. She took the donor card information and said she was going to get her little brother to try and find out who it came from."

"What?" Dex raised his voice. "Why the hell would she do that?"

I blinked, surprised that he even cared. "I don't know. She's nosey."

"Goddamn it, that's such an invasion of privacy." Dex stood up from the couch and walked to the kitchen. He opened the fridge and began to rummage around. "Do we have any beer anywhere?"

"I don't think so," I said. "Dex, what's wrong?"

He slammed the refrigerator door and walked back out to the living room wearing a pinched expression. "Nothing. I don't know, Ashley just bothers me. She's always poking her nose into other people's business."

Adrenaline pushed through my veins. "Babe, you're freaking me out."

Dex shook his head and walked over to where I was sitting on the couch. He kneeled in front of me and put his head in my lap. I exhaled and ran my fingers through his hair as a knot formed in my stomach. This was our pattern. Argue. Make up. Argue again.

"I'm sorry," he said. "I just worry she is going to try to get in between us. I know she's your friend, but I don't want her to upset you."

"It's not upsetting," I said. "I was just letting her have some fun. You know how she's obsessed with true crime and unsolved mysteries. She gets bored, and it gives her something to do."

"Exactly." Dex lifted his head. "I don't want her to rub off on you and make you paranoid or something. You remember what happened last time."

Last time. How could I forget?

"I won't." I lied, gazing into his dark eyes. "Don't worry, babe. I won't let things get out of control again. Trust me."

"I love you, Mia."

"I love you, too."

"I'm gonna go see if I can find something to drink," he said. "You want anything?"

"No, thanks. I'm good."

"Sorry again about dinner, babe. We'll make up for it this weekend."

Dex found the remnants of an old tequila bottle in the back of our cupboard, finished it off and fell asleep on the couch. I felt gross after all the work I had put into our wasted evening and wanted to take a shower. My knee was feeling surprisingly good and so far, I had only been able to give myself sponge baths. Now that I was moving around better, I felt more confident about being in the shower. I took off my knee brace, wrapped my bandaged knee in plastic cling wrap, and headed toward the bathroom. Our shower had a built-in seat, so I could easily sit and bathe myself without assistance. I needed to move slowly and take care not to slip, but otherwise, I felt like I could handle showering on my own.

I turned the water on hot and began to undress, catching my reflection in the mirror. I used to love the way I looked, vainly taking pride in my features and my body. The last few years with Dex had knocked my confidence down a bit, and before my accident, I began to obsess over my features even more. I barely recognized the person staring back at me. My mahogany hued hair was lighter now, nearly ash blonde at the roots. My once suntanned complexion had become sallow, my features sunken. Even though I was still having a hard time getting my engagement ring to unstick, I was thinner than ever. The outline of my collarbone and hips were visible in ways I had never noticed before. Even though I knew that I was frowning at my sickly reflection, my thin lips were upturned, exposing white teeth. I gasped as invisible hands wrapped around my throat again, squeezing and choking off my air supply as a voice whispered in my ear.

It's all going to be mine now.

The house.

Your body.

Your life.

Mine. Mine. Mine.

The edges of my vision grew blurry as my eyelids fluttered close. Steam fogged up the mirror as the pressure around my throat intensified. I clawed at my neck, desperate for a breath of air, but there was nothing there. I thought about my mother and father as the world went dark.

***

"Did you do something different with your hair?"

Dex cocked his head to the side as he helped me into the passenger seat of his car that following Saturday. We had an appointment to taste test wedding cake samples at Bon Vivant followed by a dinner reservation at Michelene. I was looking forward to our date night out and was feeling more energized than ever since my accident.

"No, I mean, I washed it and curled it." I flipped down the sun visor to take a look at myself in the mirror. A noticeably slimmer, paler reflection smiled back at me.

"It looks lighter," he said. "You didn't dye it?"

"No," I said. "This is just how my hair is. Does it look bad?"

"It looks great," he said. "Just different."

Dex closed the passenger door and walked around to the front. He was dressed in the same button-down and pants that he wore when he brought me flowers at my follow-up appointment. I wore a long, ankle-length dress to cover up my brace. I barely needed the crutches anymore, but I would still have to wear a supportive wrap around my knee for a while.

We drove to the bakery in silence with my hand resting on top of Dex's the entire way. My engagement ring was still stuck, despite the fact that the swelling in my hands had gone down. The dress I was wearing was loose around my waist and hips even though it had fit me perfectly before I had gone in for the procedure. Dex eyed my new shape appreciatively. Even though the hollows on my clavicle and the sharp edges of my hips were unfamiliar to me, I was beginning to feel at home in my new form.

At Bon Vivant we were greeted by the bakery owner, a woman in her mid-forties named Melanie. Her eyes sparkled behind a pair of cat eye prescription glasses and her gray streaked baby bangs and a floral A-line dress hinted at a pin-up style underneath her fitted, crisp white apron. She welcomed us and sat Dex and I down at a soda shop style round table and chairs and began to pass out samples of cake.

"So these are the ones you requested to try," Melanie said, pointing to five different plates. "This one is red velvet, that one is carrot cake. Then there's vanilla, chocolate, and my personal favorite, fruit basket."

"Oh, these all look wonderful." I speared my fork into the fruit cake sample. A gush of red syrup oozed out from between the layers of white cake and whipped cream frosting. "Can these all come in any shape and number of tiers we want?"

"Absolutely. I can customize anything you like, including the frosting and the decoration," Melanie said. "Of course, certain custom jobs will be more costly than others."

"What's the difference between buttercream and whipped cream?" I forked the bite of cake into my mouth. The frosting was so sweet the tip of my tongue began to burn.

"It's all about your preference of flavor," she said. "Though buttercream and fondant are traditional."

"I really like this one." Dex poked his finger into the whipped cream frosting. "Which one is the best for smashing cake in each other's face?"

"Dex! We are definitely not going to do that," I said, letting out a clipped laugh.

"It's tradition!" He frowned and stuck his finger in his mouth.

"I don't care, I don't like it," I said. "It's disrespectful, for one thing. Also, I'm going to spend a lot of money getting my makeup done and I don't want to get it messed up."

"Aw, you're no fun. You need to lighten up." Dex swiped his finger into the frosting again, but this time he didn't stick his finger in his mouth. This time, he dabbed a dollop of frosting on the tip of my nose. "Boop."

My molars ground together as a deeply buried synapse snapped inside my skull. The blob of frosting on the tip of my nose dripped to the floor as my entire body tremored. Without a second thought, I picked up the sample slice of red velvet cake and dumped it in his lap.

"Mia, what the fuck!" Dex jumped out of his seat as chunks of red and white cake fell from his lap. He grabbed a napkin and began to wipe away at his khaki pants, the moist cake and frosting leaving red streaks all over his groin. He stared at me with his features twisted into a contorted expression, lips sneering and eyes wide and wild.

That felt good, didn't it? A voice whispered in my ear.

He was asking for it.

He got what he deserved.

It was then that I realized I was smiling.

"See?" I said. "It isn't so nice to covered in cake."

"Have you lost your fucking *mind*?" Dex screamed.

I threw my head back and laughed.

The voice in my head laughed, too.

Chapter 8

The world was bathed in red as I watched Dex storm out of the bakery. His engine roared to life and by the time his tires squealed out of the parking lot, the color had faded. In the past, I might have felt ashamed of my actions. Instead, I only felt satisfaction. He had pushed my buttons by dismissively dabbing me with frosting and got a lap full of cake as a result. Despite my victory, I found myself without a ride, and with a mess to clean up and a bill to pay for.

"I'm sorry about that," I said, turning to Melanie. "I'll help clean up."

"It's okay." The friendly smile had been wiped off of the bakery owner's face. Her lower lip trembled as she struggled to meet my gaze. "You should probably just leave."

"I still need to pay though—"

"I'll send you a bill," she said. "Just please. Go."

"Alright."

I picked up my purse and strode out of the bakery with my head held high. I was too ashamed to call my mother and ask her to pick me up, especially after the way I had left last time. She would no doubt scold me, tell me I had been stupid to go back in the first place. I didn't want to hear it. I sat on the bench outside of the bakery and tried to consider my options. Just as I was about to call Ashley, my phone lit up with her name on the screen. I pressed the green ACCEPT CALL button and put the phone to my ear.

"I was just about to call you."

"Really? Good, I have some interesting news," she said.

I snorted and massaged the bridge of my nose. "That's funny, I have some interesting news for you, too."

"Stephen got a hit on the Cadaverbank information you gave me," she said. "I know who the donor material is from."

I sat up and my pulse began to race. "Who?"

Ashley paused for a moment, then sighed into the phone. "I think maybe it's better if I show you. Can we meet up?"

"Yeah. I'm kind of stranded at Bon Vivant right now," I said. "It's that fancy bakery I was telling you about."

"What? How?"

"I finally got Dex to come taste test wedding cakes with me. It was a disaster."

"Where is he now?"

"I don't know," I said. "I smashed a sample of red velvet cake into his lap and he stormed off."

"Oh my god," Ashley gasped. "Are you okay?"

"I'm fine. I would be grateful if you could come pick me up, though."

"Okay, give me like, five minutes and I'll be on my way," she said. "The kids are staying with my parents for the weekend. You can have Sarah's room for a few days if you need it."

"Thanks."

I ended the call and slipped the phone back in my purse. I didn't have a toothbrush or my laptop. I didn't have my therapy machines or my medicine, or even my crutches. All I had was the clothes on my back and the contents of my purse. I didn't care, though. The idea of going back to the house and facing Dex was too much. The fact was, I probably didn't need my therapy machines or medicine that much. Honestly, I didn't even need the knee brace anymore. My life may have been falling apart, but I felt stronger than ever.

As I waited for Ashley to pick me up, my thoughts drifted to what life would be like without Dex. I could get a little studio apartment again, maybe even a cat. I could take painting lessons. I could go back to school and get a new career. I could have a whole new life. Why had I been holding on so tightly to the dream of a wedding and a life with someone who clearly did not care about me?

Ashley's minivan appeared just as I was about to pull out my phone and text Dex. The instinct was always to run back to him, to always apologize, even if he was in the wrong. I didn't want to do that this time. I slipped my phone back into my bag and waved as Ashley pulled up to the curb.

"Hey, where are your crutches?"

"I left them at home," I said, opening the passenger door. "I don't really need them anymore."

"You're walking around really well," she said. "Did you dye your hair?"

I slid into the seat and closed the door. "No. Why does everyone keep asking that?"

"Mia. You're practically *blonde*. Come on, did you do it yourself? It's a pretty good dye job."

"No. I really didn't," I said. "Thank you for picking me up."

"Of course. I wanted to tell you what I found, anyway."

"What's this?"

"Stephen cracked into the Cadaverbank files. See any familiar names?"

Ashley handed me her phone. The screen was already pulled up to a website with a form showing what appeared to be medical information. I recognized the Cadaverbank logo and read through a series of numbers and information until I got to a name.

Fallon McIntyre.

How could I forget?

The hair on the back of my neck stood on end as I read the name again and again. Fallon. Fallon. Fallon. Was Fallon McIntyre really dead? Was her donated cadaver bone material really permanently grafted to my body? Of all the people in the world to die and donate their body parts, it had to be my childhood tormentor. Impossible.

"Fallon?"

"Yep," Ashley said. "The one and only."

"I have a piece of Fallon fucking McIntyre's body inside of me?"

"Seems that way," Ashley said. "I had Stephen double check. The ID numbers on the donor card match."

"No," I said. "This is impossible."

"I wish it was." Ashley pulled out of the parking lot and nodded toward her phone. "Scroll to the next page."

I tapped the screen and flipped to an obituary listing in the local paper. Ashley had really gone the extra mile when it came to her detective work.

Fallon McIntyre, age 27. Women's semi-pro PGA star and the daughter of golf legend, Willy "Mac" MacIntyre, died December 24, 2023, of drowning by misadventure. She is survived by parents, William and Kathleen MacIntyre, younger sister Sorcha and many aunts, uncles and cousins. Service will be held Jan 2 at Faith Baptist in Estero, FL.

Fallon's smiling face stared back at me from the top of the obituary. Her creamy complexion, thick blonde hair and sky-blue eyes were the very image of an all-American girl. A perfect princess. Back in the day when she would stick gum in my hair and cut me down with insults, no one believed me. To me, she was a tormentor, a dark cloud I couldn't wait to get out from under after graduation. To everyone else, she was an angel, a saint in pastel polo shirts and sneakers. She was Laura Palmer. She was Britney Spears. She was fucking *dead*.

"I can't believe this," I said, handing the phone back to Ashley. "I didn't even know she died."

"By *misadventure,*" Ashley said. "That's usually code for suicide when the family doesn't want to make it public."

"Why would she kill herself, though?" I said, glancing down at my knee. "Oh, god."

"Who knows?" Ashley said. "Fallon was a bitch in high school, and she was probably a bitch as an adult, too. She was obsessed with you and tried to make your life hell back then. Don't feel bad for one minute."

"I think I'm gonna be sick."

"Oh, shit." Ashley pulled off the road and into a gas station. The minivan screeched to a halt just in time for me to open the passenger door and empty the contents of my stomach. Fruit basket wedding cake spewed from my lips out onto the hot pavement as another body shaking tremor wracked through me. Ashley reached over into the glove compartment and pulled out a stack of paper napkins and handed me an unopened bottle of water.

"Here, sip this," she said.

I took the bottle and laughed. "You just happened to have a bottle of water?"

"Yeah, I have trail mix and some beef jerky too," she said. "I'm a mom. We always have snacks."

I took a sip of water and tried to swish the acidic flavor from my mouth. "Got any gum?"

"Of course." Ashley handed me a stick of gum from her purse. "Ready to get going again?"

"Yeah," I said. "I need to lay down."

***

When Ashley brought me to her house, I spread out on her daughter's unicorn print comforter and passed out. Between my fight with Dex and the new information regarding the origins of my donor material, I simply couldn't cope. I closed my eyes and cried until I drifted off to that space between awake and asleep, then down the rabbit hole into a dark oblivion.

That night, I didn't dream of crystal castles or fields of pink blossoms. Instead, I dreamt of blood and bone. Sinew and meat. Teeth and hair. I swam through an ocean of blood, treading to an unknown destination. The blood got in my eyes, my ears, my nose, my mouth. I woke up with the metallic taste still fresh on my tongue.

I spent all day Sunday shuffling around Ashley's house trying not to cry. I didn't feel safe, even surrounded by the familiarity of my best friend and her home, but I didn't know if I would feel safe anywhere else, either. There was something inside my body now that I did not want there. The idea of Fallon's tendons seething and taking root beneath the surface of my skin triggered a panic response that made it difficult to breathe. I wanted to go back in time and never take up jogging again. I wanted to go back to the day Dex, and I first met and tell myself to run away. What I really wanted was Fallon McIntyre's tendons out of my body.

Ashley brought me sushi, and we watched our favorite films from high school on Sunday night as I tried to recollect myself. I couldn't go home, but I couldn't stay with her forever either. I needed to break things off with Dex and move out of the house, but all the steps that it would take seemed too overwhelming. I didn't care anymore about losing wedding deposits, or what other people would think about me breaking off our engagement. Thinking about the possibility of my future away from Dex made me hopeful and nauseous all at once. All of that was overshadowed by the gruesome fact that I was using borrowed body parts from my sworn enemy.

"What if I get another doctor to do the surgery again?"

Ashley glanced over at me from her perch on the couch. Lindsay Lohan and Rachel McAdams were arguing on her television screen. A half-eaten bag of popcorn rested on the couch between us.

"Do you think you could find someone to do that?" Ashley asked.

I grabbed a handful of popcorn. "Maybe. It really freaks me out to know that the donor material was from Fallon. I don't know if I can live with it."

"I really wish I hadn't told you now," she said. "Especially with everything that's going on with Dex and healing from your surgery. It's been a tough time."

"It's okay. Part of me wanted to know," I said. "I know this sounds drastic, but I would intentionally hurt myself again just to get the tendon replaced."

"Don't do that," Ashley said. "Look, talking about self-harm is not a good sign. I think maybe it's time for you to see a professional. A counselor or something."

I nodded. "I know. I don't really mean it. Talking to a therapist wouldn't hurt, though."

"Promise me you'll call and make an appointment tomorrow?"

"I will. I need to get back to the house and get some of my things first."

"Have you talked to Dex at all?"

"No," I said. "I blocked his number. The last time I tried to leave, he brought me flowers and acted like everything was going to be okay. I need to just stay away from him. I still can't believe I dumped cake in his lap."

"Kind of a boss move." Ashley laughed. "Yeah, but that is kind of a gray area. It wasn't exactly violent, but you don't want things to get physical between the two of you."

"Exactly. And I'm so full of rage these days, I don't trust myself around him, either."

"Well, I'll go with you tomorrow to help pick up your things," Ashley said. "Just take it one step at a time."

"That's all I can do."

Ashley turned her attention back to the television. "Can you pass me the popcorn?"

"Yeah."

I reached over and passed her the bag of extra butter, theater style popcorn. Lindsay Lohan and the other mean girls got into their holiday themed chorus line on the big screen.

"Gretchen Wieners is still a pretty funny name," I said.

"What's that?"

I turned toward Ashley as she stared down at my hand. "What's what?"

"On your wrist," she said. "Is that a tattoo?"

I looked down at my left wrist. The bold outline of a monarch tattoo was clearly visible in the flashing television light.

"What in the..."

"Why didn't you tell me you got a tattoo?" Ashley whined. "I've been trying to get you to get a matching tattoo with me for, like, forever."

"I didn't," I said. "I have no idea where this came from."

"If you say so." Ashley frowned and turned back to the television.

I ran my thumb along the tattooed skin as panic crept into my chest. Something was happening to my body, and there was no more denying it. I was losing control of everything in my life — my fiancé, my home, my appearance, even my demeanor. I didn't know if a therapist was actually what I needed.

It's happening, the voice whispered.

You'll see.

Soon.

Everything will be as it should be.

Chapter 9

Monday dawned with a sky the color of blood. A late spring storm had raged all night, leaving everything wet and turning the air into a hot, humid blanket. I admired the new pink flower buds blossoming in Ashley's garden as I sipped my coffee that morning. Droplets of water clung to the blades of overgrown grass in her front yard. At the base of the tree lay a lifeless, naked baby bird, no doubt blown from his nest overnight. Part of me wanted to curl up next to the little bird and let bugs and worms and moist earth consume us both.

I couldn't hide out at my best friend's home any longer. I needed to get back to work and make an appointment with a therapist. I also needed to get some things from the house, but most importantly, I needed my laptop and my car. I could barely feel any pain in my knee anymore and felt confident enough to drive again.

Dex left for work early, so I knew that I would have plenty of time to pack my things and leave him a note. This time, there would be no going back. No return. This time we were done for good, and I was going to take better care of myself and take back my life.

Ashley drove me home that morning after I was certain

Dex had left for the day. She was reserved and polite as we ate breakfast and drank coffee, but I could sense in her body language and the clipped way she spoke to me that something felt off. As we pulled into my driveway later that morning, Ashley gazed at me from behind the wheel of her minivan with a concerned expression.

"Can I ask you something without you getting mad?"

"Sure," I said. "What?"

"Did you already know that Fallon was your donor recipient? You know, before I got the number and had Stephen look it up."

"No," I said. "How could I know?"

Ashley shrugged. "I'm not sure, it's just— "

"It's just what?"

"Your hair," she said. "The tattoo on your wrist. I looked up Fallon's Facebook account. Did you know she had a butterfly tattoo on her wrist?"

"No." I blinked, and my body went numb. "What are you trying to get at?"

Ashley exhaled in a long, exasperated sigh. "I love you, so please don't be mad. I just wonder if maybe you're going through a tough time right now and you're... I don't know, changing your style to look like Fallon?"

"Why would I ever do that?" I asked. "That sounds absolutely insane."

"It does sound very strange and far-fetched but come on Mia. You have to admit things have been weird for you lately."

"Yes, but I'm not doing any of this!" Tears sprang to my eyes. Even my own best friend thought I was overly dramatic. "I didn't dye my hair, and I didn't go out and get a tattoo. I know that I can be a bit much sometimes, but I'm not lying. Something is happening to me, and I don't know why."

Ashley sighed and stared straight ahead. "Listen, I know you don't want to run back to your parents, but the kids will be home soon. Maybe it would be best for you to stay with your folks?"

My heart sank. I really must have seemed out of my mind if she didn't want me around her kids. I couldn't blame her. I wouldn't want someone like me around my family, either.

"It's fine." I opened the passenger door.

"It's just that our house can get really noisy and wild when everyone is home. I think you would just be more comfortable somewhere else."

"Don't worry about it," I said, stepping out of her minivan. "I'll call my mom to come pick me up. Thank you."

"Promise me you'll call a therapist?" Ashley pleaded.

I nodded. "I will."

"Text me later and let me know when you're settled in with your parents, okay?"

"Okay."

I closed the door and stood in my driveway, watching as Ashley pulled away. She beeped her horn three times before speeding off. I was alone, really and truly. Ashley thought I was losing it. Dex and I were finished. My parents would take me in, but not without a good amount of sighing and headshaking. I glanced down at my wrist and rubbed at the tattoo outline. Some color was coming through on the wings now in splashes of green and blue. It wasn't going away.

You know why this is happening, the voice said.

Why even deny it?

"Shut up." My hand flew to my mouth. I had devolved to talking back to the voice in my head. Great. Things were looking worse by the minute.

I turned toward my house and walked to the front door, barely noticing the pain in my knee anymore. It had been days since I had taken any pain medication or used my physical therapy machines, yet my knee felt almost good as new. I was healing rapidly. My body shape and hair color were changing, and a tattoo was materializing on my skin like magic. There was no doubt that I was changing, and as the voice said, deep down, I knew what I was changing into.

Even though I had a lot of packing to do, I went straight to my office. It had been a long time since I cracked open my high school yearbooks, but they maintained a place of honor on my bookshelf just the same. I brought out the edition from my senior year and opened the pages to the sports section. It didn't take long for me to find Fallon McIntyre's page among the golf team's photos. Permanent marker X's blacked out her eyes and mouth, and the words SKANK, BITCH and CUNT covered every page. Fallon and I had all been so awful to each other back then, and over what? I couldn't even remember how our feud began.

I reshelved the yearbook and sat down at my desk. There was so much to do, but before I began, I hand wrote a short note to Dex. I told him that we were over, and that I would have a lawyer contact him about selling our house. I needed to begin packing a few things, but I was overwhelmed by the task and couldn't get Fallon out of my thoughts. How had she died? What were the odds that of all the people in the world, I would have been the recipient of her donor material?

As I stood from my desk, my laptop screen blipped to life and caught my attention. The tab to the "I DO!" website was open and showed that I had another message. My pulse picked up as my hand scrolled over the red icon. The message was once again from a faceless user with no name and only a series of numbers. The subject title was two words.

THE TRUTH.

I clicked the message open to see a single website link. No other message or words, just a link to an external site. I once again ignored my better instincts and clicked the link, even though it was likely spam that would infect my computer. What I saw on my laptop screen made me wish that I had a computer virus instead.

The link led me to a free porn site, one that I was unfamiliar with that had a bunch of X's in the name. The title of the video was "Petite Blonde Gets Railed at Golf Course." I swallowed and clicked the triangular play button on the center of the screen.

The video was taken with what looked like a cell phone camera on a golf course at night. The POV zoomed in on a blonde woman bent over the back of a golf cart, her bare ass exposed. The focus zoomed in to show that she was also topless.

"Put that away."

Fallon held her left hand up to cover her face, the butterfly tattoo clearly visible. My chest hurt as I covered my mouth and watched the videographer mount her from behind.

"Dammit, I said stop!" Fallon glared into the camera. "I told you, I don't want to film this anymore."

"It's okay, baby. I'll delete it afterwards."

My stomach dropped as I registered the owner of that voice. It was a voice I knew all too well.

"Dex, stop!" Fallon shouted and swiped at the cameraman.

"Shut up."

Dex's hand landed on her back, pushing her down onto the golf cart. I couldn't watch anymore. I closed out the screen and a sob ribbed through my chest. So many questions that I had about our relationship, so many gut feelings I had ignored. Dex and I were already done, but if there was any possibility that I would go back, that video had squashed it. The thought of him and her together made me sick, even more sick than the thought that part of her body was inside of me. I wanted to get out of that house and never look back. I would pack my shit and never come back. I glanced up at my dark laptop screen to close the lid and gasped.

The shadowed silhouette of a man was outlined behind me in the screen's reflection. I shrieked and turned to face the figure in the doorway.

"Wish you didn't have to find out this way, Mia," Dex said. "You know what they say. Ignorance is bliss."

Chapter 10

Scarlet waves of anger flashed before my eyes as Dex lunged at me and wrapped his hands around my throat. I struggled and pushed against him to try to get him off of me, but he was too heavy. I managed to pry one of his hands away from his grip, but it wasn't enough to get away. Spittle flew in my face as he cursed and grunted against me.

"Stay still!"

The side of my face exploded as his fist made contact with my cheek. My red-tinged vision grew hazy as my body went limp. I let go and slipped into the twilight dream sleep I had always wished for as the world began to melt away.

"She wanted so badly to be you."

Dex's voice rang in my ears as I lifted my head. My eyelids were heavy as I opened them to a blanket of blonde curls. The room was blindingly white, surrounding in a soft, focus golden glow. I was in a high school classroom, seated at a desk. In my hand was a bright pink permanent marker. I scrawled the words BITCH, CUNT, UGLY, FAT, STUPID on the desktop. The girl sitting in front of me turned around and smiled.

"Hi," Fallon said. "You're new here, right?"

I opened my mouth to speak, and a cascade of pink slime flowed from my lips.

Fuck you, I wanted to say. *Get out of my head.*

But the words didn't come. Cotton candy-colored ooze dripped from my mouth onto the desk, washing away the hateful words I had written. The strange fluid tasted like strawberry, but underneath, the flavor was foul. I gagged and spit it out.

"She wasn't even interested in me until she found out we were dating."

Dex's voice echoed through my mind and again, I was transported. This time, I was standing in a world of vibrant blue and green. A woman with blonde hair wearing a pink polo shirt and white shorts leaned up against a golf cart. She smiled and threw her head back and laughed as a man in khaki shorts spoke to her. Dex. He turned to me and glared with eyes that burned like fire.

"Fucking me was like getting back at you for everything you did to her in high school."

The vibrant world dimmed as the blue sky turned inky black. I watched as Dex forced the woman to submit to him on that same golf cart. I was there in the video, a helpless bystander. Fallon turned to face me as Dex continued to work at her from behind. Our gaze locked, and I could see that she was in pain.

Help.

Help me.

The night enveloped us all and my body catapulted through space. Dex's voice echoed through the empty void as I tumbled, tetherless and afraid.

"We got engaged, and I told her it had to stop," he said. "She didn't want it to stop."

I found myself in the back seat of Dex's car. He was behind the wheel, and Fallon was in the passenger seat. She was crying. Pleading. Dex reached across the car and smacked her with the back of his hand. Fallon opened the passenger door and ran.

The seat beneath me fell away, and I was tumbling down, down, down. A valley of leafy green trees appeared beneath my feet, and Dex's voice followed me once again.

"She found your wedding profile and told me she was going to tell you," he said, his voice a little clearer now. "She tried to get between us."

I floated through the trees and to the ground, immediately recognizing my surroundings. I had landed in the park where I jogged every day. Fallon stood beside me, hidden among the shadows, watching. I shuddered as a familiar figure jogged along the trail in the near distance. It was me, of course, wearing the same tank top and leggings I wore on the day I was injured. Just before I rounded the bend, Fallon splashed a bottle filled with a viscous fluid along the paved path. I watched, unable to stop myself, as I ran directly into her trap. I already knew what was coming next. My foot twisted on the slickened jogging path, and I heard the snap of my bones and the thud of my body as I fell to the ground. Fallon smiled and retreated further into the woods as I lay writhing.

"I told her to stop or I would release the video," Dex said, his voice now clear as day. "But she didn't stop."

Everything hurt again. My face. My wrists. My knee. I couldn't move.

I struggled to open my eyes as a ripping sound snapped me back to reality. It took me a moment to realize what was happening. Dex hovered over me with a roll of duct tape in his hands. My wrists and chest were already bound, but he hadn't gotten to my ankles yet. He leaned over and began to go to work, seemingly unaware that I had regained consciousness. Even though I was scared and barely lucid, I wasn't going to sit back and let him tie me up without a fight. Before he had a chance to grab my ankles, I kicked as hard as I could. My foot connected with his jaw and sent him tumbling back on his ass.

"Fuck!" Dex grabbed his face. His eyes were wild, and his features were twisted. I pushed at the ground, trying to roll the office chair away from him as I wiggled against my binds. It was no use, though. He had secured my wrists too tight.

"I knew from the moment you came home that she was with you." Dex chuckled and rose to his feet. "I could hear her and smell her... fuck! You even taste like her."

"Let me go!" I screamed, still unable to free myself.

"See, that's the thing. I don't want to let you go. Fallon was a mistake. I knew that from the start." The overhead light dimmed and flickered. Dex stood to his feet. "I had to stop her. I did it for us, Mia. Don't you see that?"

"Did what?"

Something moved in the doorway. From the corner of my eye, I thought I had seen a flash of pink. A blur of blonde.

You know, the voice said.

You know what he did to me.

"You killed her, didn't you?" Bile stung the lining of my throat as I struggled not to heave. "Oh, god. You killed her."

"I solved our problem," Dex said, his lips set in a half frown. "She loved drugs just as much as she loved golf. It wasn't hard to make it look like she overdosed."

"Why?" I cried, still choking on my own stomach acid. "You're so fucked up."

"Me? I'm the fucked up one?" Dex let out an explosive laugh. "That's a good one. She told me what you and Ashley did to her. You're no saint."

The words stung like another punch to the cheek. "I'm not a murderer, though."

“I did it for us,” he said. “Look, you’re upset right now. You’re not thinking straight because that thing inside of you is infecting your mind.”

“What?”

“She’s trying to get between us again. But I won’t let her.”

Dex opened the desk drawer where I kept my wedding scrap-book supplies. He rummaged through my perfectly organized selection of colored markers and pens and pulled out a slim silver tool and a roll of duct tape. My heart sank. I already knew what was coming next.

“Stop,” I pleaded. “Dex, you don’t have to do this.”

I screamed as Dex ripped a long length of tape from the spool and wrapped it around my head.

“Help!”

My words were muffled as the same tape that was wrapped around my wrists cut off my voice. Dex knelt in front me, uncapped the tip of my x-acto blade and examined the cutting tool. The sharp tip glinted in the flickering overhead light.

“The only way to fix this thing between us is to remove the problem,” he said. “We’re going to cut her out of you.”

Bright blooms of scarlet burst forth against my unusually fair complexion as Dex sank the tip of the blade into my skin. The surgical incision site had healed over so well in such a short time that the scar was barely visible, but now a new mark would take its place. The pain was sharp and focused, a searing line of agony. I was helpless. I could not move, could not fight. Dex had even taped my mouth shut so that I could not scream. I was trapped inside myself in a helpless state of agony.

“I know what you’re thinking.” Dex paused his work and pressed the gauze against the wound. “You think this won’t work, right? Well, if I’m honest, I’m not so sure it will work either."

I whimpered, my voice muffled against the duct tape covering my mouth.

Please.

Stop.

"The thing is, we'll never get another doctor to agree to give you a new replacement," he said. "But I need to know first that this will take care of our problem. So, I'll remove this tainted ligament and we'll make it look like you had another accident. Then once you're back to your old self again, we can fix you up with a brand-new knee."

Dex returned to his work, and I let out another muffled scream.

"Pain is purifying," he said. "I love you Mia, and I would have gladly given you medication for this. But Fallon is just too comfortable taking over your body. We need to get her out."

Fallon.

My head snapped back as he said her name.

The pain in my knee subsided as icy tendrils spread through my veins. The cold sensation crept up my thighs and spread through my chest. It snaked up my neck and seeped into my skull, chilling me to the core. Fingernails of ice sank into my brain, and everything went black. I swam through the dark toward a small light. I saw myself standing in the doorway, staring at Dex's back. The person in the chair looked like me, but different somehow. Her blue eyes met mine among a tangle of blonde hair and duct tape. I glanced down at my hands — or rather, where they should be — and saw nothing but air. I glanced back up at Fallon, and her eyes pleaded at me again. Could she see me?

The golf clubs, the voice said.

The voice. *Fallon's* voice. It had been her speaking to me

the entire time, but of course it had. Working against me. Sabotaging me. Trying to steal my life. Now she wanted me to help her? For all the hatred I held in my heart, all the long-held anger and animosity, in that moment, all I felt for her was pity. Dex had stolen her life and now he was going to hurt her again.

Hit him over the head.

I turned toward Dex's golf bag slumped in the corner of the office. His bent golf clubs stuck out the top in awkward angles.

"How?" I asked. My voice sounded strange. Hollow. Wisp-like. "I have no hands."

You can do anything, she said. *You can bend golf clubs. Tear apart binders. Just try.*

I reached out an invisible hand and wrapped my fingers around Dex's favorite nine iron. To my surprise, I lifted it out of the bag with ease. Fallon let out another muffled scream as Dex continued to work at her knee.

"Almost there," he said. "Just another minute and you'll have this cursed piece of flesh out of you for good."

I drew the club back over my shoulder. I thought about all the times Dex and I had gone golfing together, and about all the details of our wedding that would never happen. I thought about the video he took of him and Fallon together. I used every ounce of energy left in my ethereal form and swung.

The head of the club connected with Dex's temple, making a cracking sound not unlike a wooden bat hitting a baseball. He let out a sound somewhere between a gurgle and a grunt and fell to the floor. I dropped the club as he convulsed, blood pouring from his ear.

Help me.

Fallon stared at me with those pleading eyes. I moved toward her and ripped off the duct tape from her mouth and hands. The x-acto knife laid in an ever-growing pool of blood at her feet. Even though Dex had damaged her knee with his shoddy surgery, the wound already appeared to be healing.

"Thank you," Fallon said. "I'm so sorry."

"I'm sorry, too," I said, my disembodied voice a little stronger now. "For everything."

"We need to work fast," she said. "I can't clean this up on my own."

I glanced down at Dex and nudged him with my foot. It was difficult to feel sorry for him. I had sunk to his level. I was a murderer now.

"Give me back my body first," I said.

A thin-lipped smile spread across her face. "Or else what?"

"Or else I'll haunt you, too."

"Fine," Fallon said, blowing a mass of blonde bangs from her brow. "But we have to share."

Epilogue

One Month Later

"Should we do two miles today, or three?"

I stretched my arms over my head toward the sky and looked out over the entrance to my favorite jogging path. It was a glorious late spring morning, though if one didn't know any better, they would think it was summer. I liked the heat, though. It made me sweat and reminded me that I was alive.

Three, Fallon said, her voice resonating in the space between my ears. *I need to stretch my legs.*

"*Our* legs," I corrected her.

I took a deep breath and glanced at my hands as I reached for my toes. Each wrist now featured a butterfly tattoo — one for me, and one for my new friend. Over the last few weeks, as we learned the mechanics of our new shared situation, I had come to realize that Fallon and I weren't so different after all. We enjoyed a lot of the same things, and she had a wicked sense of humor. Terrible taste in men, though.

What should we have for dinner tonight? Fallon asked. *Sushi? Pizza?*

"Neither. You made a date with Jeremy from the dating app, remember? He's taking us to that fancy restaurant."

Right. He was the one with the nice smile.

"Don't you think it's a little too soon to be dating? We don't want to look suspicious."

A couple of retired women in workout wear and sneakers fast-walked by as we continued to talk to each other out loud. They frowned at me and shook their heads as they passed, their pants swishing and arms pumping. People gave us a lot of strange looks at the park, at the golf course and at the grocery store, but we paid no mind. Fallon and I had become more like roommates and best friends than anything else. I was wrong to think that ripping Fallon's cadaver material out of me would have been the right thing to do. Sure, it was inconvenient to have to share a body with another woman, but it was worth it. Together, we were stronger. Faster. Smarter. Together, we were perfect.

I glanced out at the lake next to the jogging path. A crested night heron stared back at me with its beady, accusatory eyes. Did it know that Fallon and I had dumped our fiancé in the middle of that very lake? No one had doubted our story so far. The philandering fiancé. The revenge porn video. A mysterious withdrawal of funds from his account. The authorities seemed satisfied with the notion that he had disappeared, likely hiding in another country. We were safe, for now.

You know, maybe we should just cancel the date, Fallon said. *We can have a girls' night in! Order pizza and watch a movie instead.*

I smiled and secured my blonde hair into a ponytail. I was getting used to my new features. I didn't look exactly like my old self anymore, but I didn't look exactly like Fallon either. We had become something new. Something stronger. Something better.

"I'd like that," I said. "On second thought, let's put this knee to the test. Wanna go for four miles?"

Fallon's voice cackled inside my head. *Make it five.*

I smiled and took my position. "You're on."

Afterword

Content Warnings

Surgery, emotional abuse, physical abuse, suicide, murder, rape, animal carcass, body horror

About the Author

Wendy Dalrymple loves to explore the beauty in horrific things. When she's not writing femme-focused #pinkhorror, you can find her hiking with her family, painting (bad) wall art, and trying to grow as many pineapples as possible. Follow her at Instagram and TikTok @wendydalrymplewrites.

You can connect with me on:

- https://linktr.ee/wendydalrymple
- https://twitter.com/wendy_dalrymple

Also by Wendy Dalrymple

Parasocial
Casey is nineteen, struggling and social media obsessed. When her favorite StreamVid star, Della, falls ill, Casey takes it upon herself to set up a fund to foot her medical bills. However, when Casey's online obsession bleeds into her IRL world, things go sideways and it becomes all too clear that Della might not be who she seems.

PARASOCIAL is a Florida Gothic meditation on obsession, social media, and the lengths people will go to achieve online success

White Ibis

"Truly terrifying" - Jenna Dietzer, author of "The Lovebugs"

"Creepy as hell" - Sheri L. Williams, author of "Forest of Blood'

OBSESSION. LIES. GREED.

Chelsea is vain, self-absorbed, and driven in life only by want and her obsession with being the best. Even though she is desperate to portray an outwardly perfect image, things are far from perfect at home.

One day at yoga class, Chelsea meets a woman named Damaris who is exactly like her; beautiful, confident, and reaching high to be her best self. Damaris and Chelsea become instant best friends and bond over healthy eating, fitness, and their love of luxury items. As Chelsea's heart hardens toward her boyfriend, her obsession with the enigmatic Damaris only blossoms.

As one bad decision turns into another, Chelsea begins to think she is being followed by a white bird. Her new best friend Damaris suggests a girls' weekend in New Orleans to get away from it all and Chelsea readily agrees. Unfortunately for Chelsea, it soon becomes clear that she can't run away from her problems and instead finds herself tumbling head-first into a downward spiral

Milton Keynes UK
Ingram Content Group UK Ltd.
UKHW020749240724
446081UK00001B/26